MY FIRST LITTLE HOUSE BOOKS

ADAPTED FROM THE LITTLE HOUSE BOOKS

By Laura Ingalls Wilder

Illustrated by Jody Wheeler

HARPERCOLLINS PUBLISHERS

To Rodney Harold

—J.W.

Special thanks to Wendy Smith, Pat Guilmette, and Pat's young oxen, Bart and Ben.

A Farmer Boy Birthday *Text adapted from* Farmer Boy, *copyright 1933, copyright renewed 1961, Roger Lea MacBride. Illustrations copyright © 1998 by Renée Graef. Art direction by Renée Graef. Printed in the U.S.A.* *http://www.harperchildrens.com Library of Congress Cataloging-in-Publication Data Wilder, Laura Ingalls, 1867–1957. A farmer boy birthday / adapted from the Little House books by Laura Ingalls Wilder ; illustrated by Jody Wheeler. p. cm. — (My first Little house books) Summary: Almanzo Wilder celebrates his birthday by breaking in a pair of calves and sledding on his new sled. ISBN 0-06-027476-X. — ISBN 0-06-027477-8 (lib. bdg.) 1. Wilder, Almanzo—Juvenile Fiction. [1. Wilder, Almanzo—Fiction. 2. Birthdays—Fiction. 3. Farm life—Fiction.] I. Wheeler, Jody, ill. II. Title. III. Series. PZ7.W6461Fat 1998 97-18664 [E]—dc21 CIP AC 1 2 3 4 5 6 7 8 9 10 ❖ First Edition HarperCollins®, ®, and Little House® are trademarks of HarperCollins Publishers Inc.*

Illustrations for the My First Little House Books are
inspired by the work of Garth Williams with his
permission, which we gratefully acknowledge.

Once upon a time, a little boy named Almanzo lived in a farmhouse in the New York State countryside. He lived with his father, his mother, his big brother, Royal, and his big sisters, Eliza Jane and Alice.

One winter morning Almanzo was eating his good, hot oatmeal when Father said, "It's your birthday, son." Almanzo had forgotten! Now he would not have to go to school. "There's something for you in the woodshed," Father said. So Almanzo ate his oatmeal as fast as he could.

At last breakfast was over, and Almanzo and Father went to the woodshed. Inside there was a little calf-yoke for Almanzo's own two calves, Star and Bright. Father had made the yoke himself, and it was strong and light. Father said to Almanzo, "Son, you are old enough now to break those calves."

Almanzo carried the little yoke to the barn, and Father walked beside him. Star and Bright were in their warm stall. When they saw Almanzo, they licked him with their wet, rough tongues. They did not know that he was going to teach them how to behave like big grown oxen.

Almanzo and Father led the calves into the snowy barnyard. Father helped Almanzo fit the yoke over the two calves.

When Father had tied a rope around Star's little horn, he said, "Well, son, I'll leave you to figure it out." Then Almanzo knew he was really old enough to do important things all by himself.

Almanzo stood in the snow and looked at the calves, and the calves looked back at him. He thought about how he could make the calves understand that when he said, "Giddap!" they must walk straight ahead, and when he said, "Whoa!" they must stop. Finally he went to the cows' feed-box and filled his pockets with carrots.

"Giddap!" he shouted. Then he showed Star and Bright a carrot. The calves came forward at once. "Whoa!" shouted Almanzo when they reached him. They stopped for the carrot. Almanzo gave each of them a piece. How quickly they learned!

Almanzo practiced and practiced until the calves were behaving just like grown-up oxen. When Father came to the barn door and said, “It’s dinner-time, son,” Almanzo could hardly believe it. The whole morning had gone by in a minute.

Father, Mother, and Almanzo ate dinner in the kitchen instead of the dining room. Almanzo thought it was very strange to be eating alone with Father and Mother, without Royal and Alice and Eliza Jane. When he was finished eating, Mother said, "Please fill the wood-box, Almanzo."

Almanzo opened the woodshed door by the stove. And there, right before him, was a new hand-sled! Almanzo could hardly believe it was for him. So he asked, "Whose sled is that, Father?"

Mother laughed and Father twinkled his eyes. "Do you know any other boy here that wants it?" Father asked.

It was very cold out, but the sun was shining. All afternoon Almanzo played with his sled. He climbed to the top of the hill and away he went. Each time the sled went flying end over end into the deep drifts, Almanzo went flying too. Then he pulled the sled up the hill again for another ride.

When Almanzo was tired of sledding, he came back to the warm house for apples and doughnuts and cookies. In his right hand he held a doughnut, and in his left hand he held a cookie. He took a bite of one, then the other. Then he climbed the stairs to Father's attic workroom.

Father was making shingles from pieces of oak logs. His hands moved smoothly and quickly. They did not stop even when he looked up and said, "Be you having a good time, son?" Almanzo answered, "Father, can I do that?" So Father put his big hands over Almanzo's, and together they shaved one side of a shingle smooth and then the other.

Then Almanzo went to watch Mother weave cloth on her loom. Mother was sitting at the big loom. Her hands were flying and her right foot was tapping on the treadle. Thud! said the treadle. Clackety-clack! said the shuttle. Thump! said the hand-bar, and back flew the shuttle. Everything was snug and comfortable.

Too soon the shadows slanted down the eastward slopes. Royal and Eliza Jane and Alice came home from school, and the four of them all finished chores together as usual. Almanzo's happy birthday had come to an end, but what a wonderful day it had been.